The Sun Robbers

The Sun Robbers

GUS CLARKE

Andersen Press · London

First published in 2000 by
Andersen Press Limited,
20 Vauxhall Bridge Road, London SW1V 2SA

British Library Cataloguing in Publication Data available
ISBN 0-86264-954-4

Printed and bound in Great Britain
by Mackays of Chatham plc, Chatham, Kent

For A.M.U.K.

Rabbit opened his eyes and sat up. He turned on the light and looked at his watch. It was ten past eight.

He jumped out of bed, washed, dressed, made toast, ate toast, brushed his teeth, combed his hair, put on his shoes, opened the door, turned off the light, closed the door...

...and fell down the steps.

Rabbit sat still for a while and rubbed his head. And his eyes. Then he got up and ran as fast as he could to Big Dog's house and banged on the door.

'Open the door, Big Dog,' he shouted. He banged on the window. 'Open the door, Big Dog!'

Big Dog opened the window.

'What's all the noise?' asked Big Dog. 'It's the middle of the night.'

'It's not,' said Rabbit. 'It's half past eight. And why aren't you dressed? Get up, quick! Someone has stolen the sun!'

Big Dog got up, quick. There was no time to lose. Something would have to be done. He looked up at the sky. It was dark, very dark. Rabbit was right. Someone had stolen the sun.

'What shall we do?' asked Big Dog.

'Catch them,' said Rabbit. 'Catch them and make them put it back. Hurry up. They won't have got far.'

Big Dog ran. He ran fast.

Big Dog stopped. He ran back.
'Which way did they go?' he asked.

Rabbit looked at the sky and narrowed his eyes. He licked his finger and held it up in the air.

'Don't know,' he said. 'We must look for clues. Search for a trail. We'll need help.' He looked around him. 'Where *is* everyone?'

'They'll all be in bed,' said Big Dog. 'Like me.'

Rabbit tutted. 'Then wake them up,' he said.

Big Dog ran off again.

Rabbit sat down on a log. Someone would have to take charge. He closed his eyes and thought for a minute. He opened his eyes.

'Yes,' he said. '*I* shall take charge.'

Big Dog was having trouble at sheep's house. She wouldn't open the window and couldn't hear a word he was saying. Then Baa Lamb woke up and started crying. Big Dog gave up and went across the road to tell Pig.

Pig let him in straight away. She was surprised to hear about the sun but if that was what Rabbit had said she could well believe it. She looked across at the big clock on the sideboard. It must have stopped in the middle of the night.

'Rabbit knows best,' she said.
'Come on,' said Big Dog. 'He's waiting for us.'

They both hurried over to Badger's.
He was up anyway so it didn't take
him long to put on his hat and coat.

Big Dog left it to Pig and Badger to go and tell the Goats while he set off for the Hen House. Rooster was very upset. He'd been fast asleep and just couldn't believe it at first. But he had to. Rabbit was never wrong.

The hens didn't really understand but said they'd come along anyway. Big Dog thought perhaps it would be better if they didn't and Rooster agreed.

Meanwhile, back at the log, Rabbit was thinking hard. He was taking charge and when Big Dog came back with the others he would have to tell them what to do. So he was thinking hard.

'Hello, young Rabbit,' said a crinkly voice. 'And what are *you* doing up so early?'

Rabbit looked up. It was Elderly Owl.

'Hello, Elderly,' said Rabbit. 'But I'm not doing anything up so early.' And he told him what had happened to the sun.

'And when Big Dog gets back with all the others we're going to catch the robbers and make them put it back,' said Rabbit. 'I'm taking charge.'

Elderly Owl looked over his glasses
and down at Rabbit. He said
nothing, but stroked his chin with the
tip of his wing.

'Rabbit,' he said at last. 'What was
the time when you woke up?'

'About ten past eight,' said Rabbit.
'I looked at my watch.'

The owl took off his glasses and
said nothing. He looked up at the sky
and then down at Rabbit.

'Rabbit,' said Elderly Owl. 'Why are
you wearing your watch upside
down?'

Rabbit looked at his watch. And
then at the owl. Then back at his
watch. Even in this light he could see
that Elderly was right. The watch was
upside down.

'Rabbit,' said Elderly Owl. 'What is the time now?'

Rabbit looked at his watch.

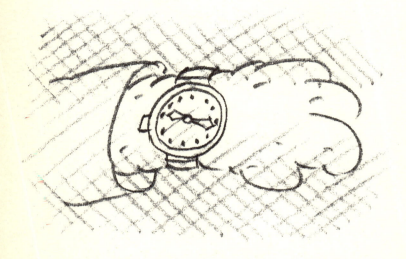

'It's a quarter past nine,' he said.

'Rabbit,' said Elderly Owl. 'Take off your watch and put it back on the other way up.'

Rabbit did as he was told.

'Rabbit,' said Elderly Owl. 'What is the time now?'

Rabbit looked carefully at his watch again.

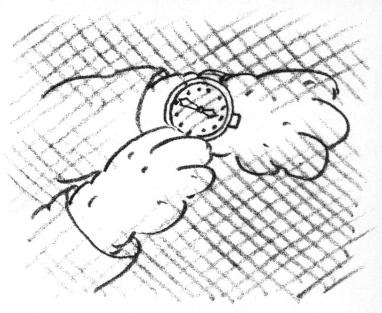

'It's a quarter to three…' he said.
He looked up at the owl. Then back
at the watch. '…Oh dear.'

'I'm afraid so,' said the owl.

'So when I woke up and my watch
said it was ten past eight,' said
Rabbit. 'It was really…' He stopped.
He couldn't work it out.

'Twenty to two,' said Elderly Owl.

'Oh dear,' said Rabbit again. 'Oh
dear, oh dear, oh dear.'

Pig and Badger were having a difficult time with the Goats. They weren't at all pleased at being woken up and quite frankly didn't believe a word of it. It was only when Big Dog and Rooster arrived to see

what was keeping them that they were finally convinced. But it didn't make them any happier about it. Big Dog was in a hurry to get everybody back to where he'd left Rabbit but the Goats wouldn't keep up and grumbled every step of the way.

By the time they got there Elderly Owl had worked out a plan to help Rabbit out of the mess he had got himself into. At first he had wanted Rabbit to own up and tell the truth to the others. But Rabbit didn't want to. He said they'd all think he was very silly and not believe anything he said ever again. Elderly agreed that this was very likely.

Everyone was pleased to see Elderly Owl. They knew he was a clever old bird and were glad to have his help in tracking down the sun robbers. Also he could fly, which was useful.

'Hello, all,' said Elderly and held up his hand for silence. 'Rabbit has told me all about the robbers. And all about his plan to catch them. Please listen to Rabbit,' he said. 'Rabbit is in charge.'

Rabbit cleared his throat. 'This is my plan,' he said.

'**F**irst,' said Rabbit, 'we'll make two teams. Big Dog will lead one team. And I will lead the other.'

'OK,' said Big Dog. 'You pick first.'

'Big Dog,' said Rabbit sternly, 'this is not a game of football. This is serious.'

'Sorry, Rabbit,' said Big Dog.

'And anyway,' said Rabbit, 'I've already picked. You can have Pig. And Badger. And Rooster. And the Goats,' he said. 'And I'll have Owl.' That sounded pretty good to Big Dog.

One of the Goats started to ask why
there were six in one team and only
two in the other. But Rabbit
interrupted him.

'*Second,*' he said, 'you will go that
way.' He pointed to the west.

'And we,' he said, pointing to the
east, 'will go this way.'

The other Goat wanted to ask why nobody was going north and nobody was going south but Rabbit interrupted again.

'*Third*,' he said, 'we'll catch the sun robbers and make them put it back.'

Elderly Owl coughed.

'...Or you will,' said Rabbit.

The Goats were about to ask how exactly they were supposed to do that. But Rabbit was gone.

'Come on,' said Big Dog. 'Let's get going. This way,' and ran off.

The Goats didn't move. They weren't happy. Apart from anything else, they'd only just come from that way - they might as well have stayed where they were and had an extra half hour in bed.

Pig and Badger did their best to hurry them up. Big Dog had disappeared into the darkness.

'Come *on!*' called Big Dog. 'Keep up. We'll never catch them at this rate.'

Pig and Badger gave up on the Goats and set off towards the sound of Big Dog.

'Wait for us then,' said the Goats, following close behind. The sooner the whole thing was over and done with the happier they would be. Pig and Badger doubted it.

Rooster flapped along at the back in silence. He couldn't understand why he felt so tired. He was usually up and about and feeling fine by this time of the morning...

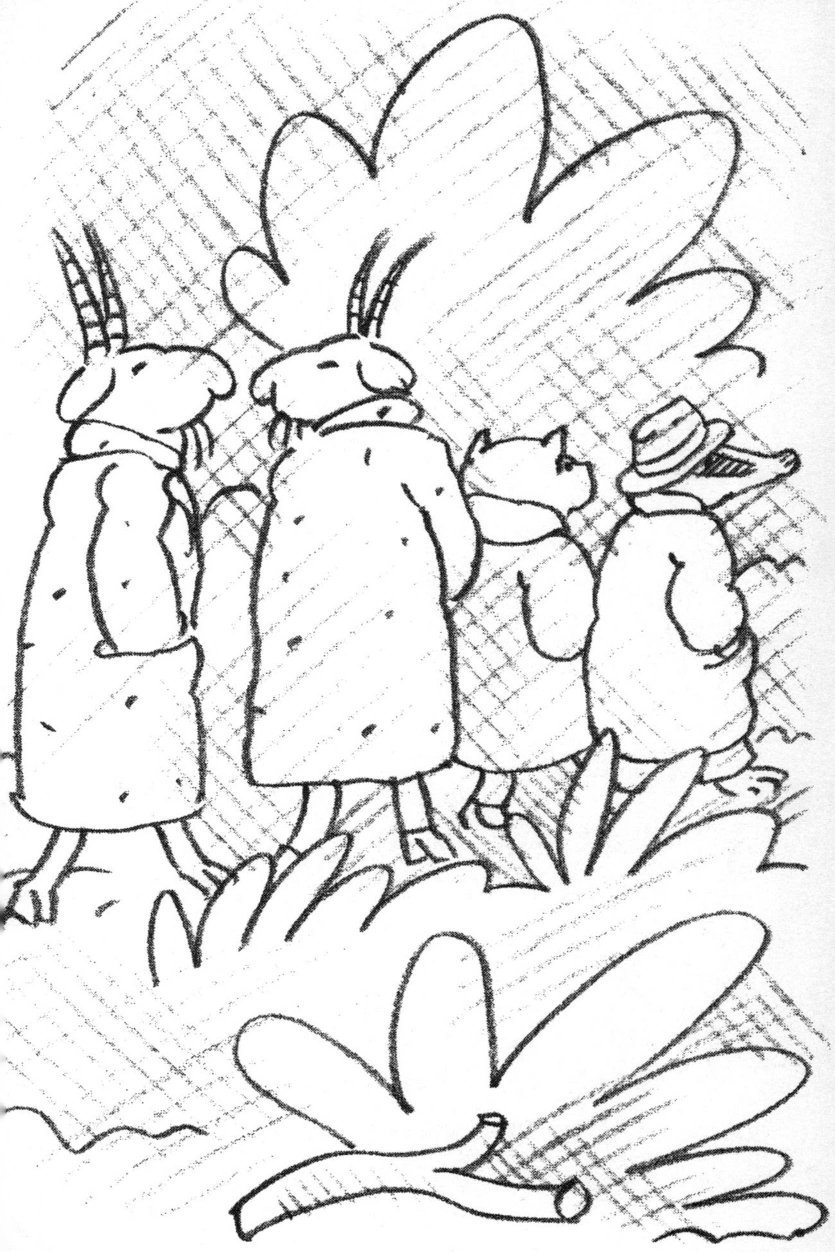

Rabbit and Elderly Owl hadn't gone very far themselves when the owl stopped. He made himself comfortable on a low branch and waited for Rabbit to catch up.

'This will do,' he said. Elderly Owl took off his glasses and rubbed his eyes. Then he closed them.

Rabbit hopped nervously from foot to foot.

'What shall *I* do?' he said.

'Stop hopping,' said Elderly. 'And wait.'

Rabbit stopped hopping. He sat down and stared hard into the darkness in front of him. And waited.

Big Dog, Pig, Badger and Rooster tip-toed past the Hen House. They'd been very pleased when the Goats had made up their minds to go straight home and have no more to do with this sun robber business. They'd had more than enough of the Goats and would get on a lot better without them.

Rooster had planned to stop and look in on the Hen House to see that all was well but the others had persuaded him not to. They'd only just got rid of one problem and didn't want another.

None of them really knew what
they would do if they caught up with
the robbers but didn't like to say so.
Pig hoped they wouldn't be very big.
Perhaps she could roll on top of them
and squash them. Once they were
safely past the hens she tried out one
or two of her fiercest grunts and
snorts.

'Bless you,' said Badger.

Badger was hoping they wouldn't
be too quick for him. He'd got some
very useful claws if he could get close
enough. He stopped to examine
them.

'Got a splinter?' said Rooster.
Rooster didn't know *what* he would
be able to do. He could look quite big
and tough if he fluffed up his
feathers. It impressed the hens
anyway. And then there were his

wings. Perhaps he could fly around
the robbers and flap his wings in
their faces. *That* would frighten them.
He hadn't really had much practice
at flying but he knew he could do it if
he tried. Once he had jumped off the
Hen House roof and flown all the way
to the ground. He tried a few big
flaps.

'Steady on,' said Big Dog and
helped Rooster to his feet.

Big Dog thought the best thing he could do was to do what he did best - run around and make a lot of noise. He'd upset a lot of people that way in the past so it was worth a try. As long as he didn't have to bite anyone. He wasn't very good at that. Everyone always said his bark was worse than his bite. And they were right.

Suddenly Big Dog stood still.
'Shhh!' he said. 'I can hear them.
Listen...'

'**R**abbit,' said Elderly Owl, opening one eye. 'What's the time?'

Rabbit studied his watch. 'Ten to five,' he said.

Elderly stood up and stretched his wings slowly. Then he launched himself off the branch and flew up into the darkness above. He aimed for the top of the tallest tree and perched as lightly as he could. The owl looked up at the stars then turned his head to the east.

'Right on time,' he said to himself.
There was an unmistakable glow, low
down on the horizon in the distance.

Elderly flew back down to the
branch above Rabbit. Rabbit looked
up hopefully. 'Is it?' he asked.

'It is,' said Elderly. 'I'll go and find
the others.'

He stretched his wings again.

'And, Rabbit,' said Elderly, 'you can
hop if you like.'

Rabbit hopped.

Big Dog, Pig, Badger and Rooster stood still and listened.

'There it is,' said Big Dog.

'I can't hear a thing,' said Pig.

'Nor me,' said Rooster. 'Can you, Badger?'

'Not a sausage,' said Badger. 'Sorry, Pig.'

'*Listen!*' said Big Dog.

They listened.

'There it is,' whispered Big Dog in a tiny voice. '*They're behind us!*'

They spun round and stared into the darkness, frozen in terror. They could all hear it now - a terrible whooshing noise filled the air. And it was getting closer.

Pig ran behind Big Dog and held
on tight. Badger ran behind Pig and
held on tight. Rooster ran behind
Badger and held on tight.

Big Dog stepped back. So did Pig.
Badger stepped back. Rooster didn't.
Big Dog, Pig and Badger fell in a
heap on top of Rooster.

They all covered their eyes - except
for Rooster, who couldn't reach his.

Elderly Owl landed with a bump on the ground next to them.

'What happened?' he said.

The heap muttered and mumbled and struggled to its feet - except for Rooster, who couldn't find his.

'Come on,' said Elderly. 'We've got to get back to Rabbit.' He told them how he had seen the sun in the distance and had left Rabbit all on his own.

'Did you see the robbers?' asked Big Dog.

'Are they big?' asked Pig.

'Are there lots?' asked Badger.

'Are they fierce?' asked Rooster.

But Elderly Owl had no time for questions. He was up in the air and flapping hard. 'Come *on!*' he screeched.

'They must be big,' said Pig.

'There must be lots,' said Badger.

'And terribly fierce,' said Rooster.

'Poor Rabbit,' said Big Dog. 'He'll need our help.'

'There's no time to lose,' said Badger.

Rooster was still feeling a bit squashed so Pig helped him up for a piggyback. And they all set off to help poor Rabbit.

Rabbit was hopping with happiness. The sun was climbing up over the horizon and into the sky. Everything was going to be all right.

He took off his jacket, loosened his tie and bent down to rub just a little bit of dust into his fur. Then he chose a comfortable clump of grass and lay down.

'**C**ock-a-doodle-doooo!' crowed
Rooster, bouncing up and down
on Pig's back. He couldn't help
himself, he was so excited.

The sun was back up in the sky!

Daylight was creeping into the
woods and lighting up the path in
front of them. Big Dog was running
up and down ahead, desperate to get
there but not *too* much before the
others - just in case. Badger was
doing his best to keep up.

Elderly Owl sat waiting on a low branch at the edge of the clearing where Rabbit lay still. 'Over here!' called the owl. 'Quick!'

Big Dog, Badger, Pig and Rooster burst into the open shouting and cheering.

'Well done, Rabbit!'
'Hooray for Rabbit!'
'Rabbit's done it!'
'Good old Rabbit!'

Then they saw Rabbit on his clump of grass.

'Rabbit!' 'What happened?' 'Are you all right?' 'Wake up!' they cried and rushed over. Elderly Owl joined them. 'Oh dear,' he said.

Rabbit stirred, sat up and held his head.

'Where am I?' he said and looked around him. 'What happened?'

Big Dog told Rabbit about the Sun Robbers stealing the sun.

'Did they?' said Rabbit. 'I don't remember.'

Pig told Rabbit how he had worked out a plan to catch them and make them put it back.

'Did I?' said Rabbit.

Badger told Rabbit how he must have been hurt in the terrible struggle.

'Was I?' said Rabbit.

And Rooster just told him how he must be so very, very brave.

'Am I?' said Rabbit.

'Rabbit,' they said, 'you're a hero.'

Rabbit blushed. 'Really?' he said.

Elderly Owl looked over his glasses and down at Rabbit. And said nothing.

It was going to be a long day. Elderly Owl suggested that after all the excitement they should go home for a short nap. He was going to have one himself.

The owl flew back to the low branch and made himself comfortable. In the distance he could hear Big Dog, Pig, Badger and Rooster chattering to each other as they made their way home. But he couldn't hear Rabbit.

The voices grew fainter and then all was quiet. Elderly Owl closed his eyes and went to sleep.

But not for long.

'Elderly,' said a small voice from below. 'Are you awake?'

Elderly Owl woke with a start and looked down. It was Rabbit.

'Elderly,' said Rabbit, 'I can't sleep.'

'And why is that, young Rabbit?' asked the owl.

Rabbit shuffled from foot to foot. 'I'm not a hero,' he said. 'I'm just a silly rabbit.'

Elderly Owl looked down kindly. 'I know,' he said. 'So what will you do?'

Rabbit stared hard at the ground.
'I'll tell them the truth,' he said.
'After all,' he looked up hopefully at
the owl, 'anyone can make a
mistake, can't they?'

Elderly Owl looked over his glasses
and smiled down at Rabbit.

'Rabbit,' he said. 'Now you really
are a hero.'

Other titles in the TIGERS series

Damon Burnard
REVENGE OF THE KILLER VEGETABLES
In his mania to win the annual vegetable show, Curly's Dad unleashes gigantic man-eating vegetables onto the town's festivities. Can Curly save the day and her dad?
'All great fun' *Books for Keeps*

0 86264 526 3   80pp   £5.99 cased

Gus Clarke
CAN WE KEEP IT, DAD?
When a cute little stray kitten is found in the park and brought home, the whole family is delighted. Well, almost . . . they're not quite sure about Dad.
'A gem of a chapter book' *T. E. S*

0 86264 871 8   64pp   £7.99 cased

Ann Jungman
DRACULA IS BACKULA
Count Dracula's castle is falling to pieces and he desperately needs to raise some money for repairs. So he decides to seek his fortune in England, starring in vampire films . . .

0 86264 894 7   64pp   £7.99 cased

Kara May
CAT'S WITCH AND THE LOST BIRTHDAY
Illustrated by Doffy Weir
The fourth story in the popular series about Aggie Witch and Cat.When Aggie Witch forgets the date of her birthday she decides to go on strike until she finds it - to the alarm of the Wantwichers who need her magic, and to the annoyance of Cat, who decides to leave home.

0 86264 532 3   64pp   £5.99 cased

Barbara Mitchelhill
ERIC AND THE STRIPED HORROR
Illustrated by Bridget MacKeith
A parcel from South America! Eric couldn't wait to find out what was inside, but when he did, extraordinary things started to happen . . .
'The characters are wonderfully written and the illustrations leap off the page' *School Librarian*

0 86264 672 3   80pp   £6.99 cased

ERIC AND THE WISHING STONE
Illustrated by Bridget MacKeith
Eric is in deep trouble at school since his brain power returned to normal
after the artificial stimulation of the Striped Horror. But then another
present arrives from South America. The second amusing tale of Eric and
the adventures that befall him!

0 86264 848 3   80pp   £7.99 cased

ERIC AND THE PIMPLE POTION
Illustrated by Bridget MacKeith
Eric's spots are multiplying. Dare he use the exotic face cream Auntie Rose
has sent from South America? When he tries out the pimple potion he soon
discovers there are terrible side effects.

0 86264 963 3   80pp   £7.99 cased

Cara Lockhart Smith
THE WITCH-BABY
Illustrated by Bridget MacKeith
When Sophie agrees to look after a witch-baby for the day, she soon finds
she has taken on more than she had bargained for!
'A lively tale for newly confident readers' *Kids Out*
Featured in Book Trust's *100 Best Books 1999*.

0 86264 800 9   80pp   £3.99 paperback